Don't Cook Cinderella

FRANCESCA SIMON

Illustrated by Tony Ross

Orion
Children's Books

Don't Cook Cinderella is available on CD,
read by Simon Russell Beale

First published in Great Britain in 1996
as *Big Class, Little Class*
by Orion Children's Books
a division of the Orion Publishing Group Ltd
Orion House
5 Upper St Martin's Lane
London WC2H 9EA

An Hachette UK Company

11 13 15 17 19 20 18 16 14 12

Text © Francesca Simon 1996, 2005
Illustrations © Tony Ross 2005

The Orion Publishing Group's policy is to use papers that
are natural, renewable and recyclable products and
made from wood grown in sustainable forests. The logging
and manufacturing processes are expected to conform to
the environmental regulations of the country of origin.

A catalogue record for this book is available
from the British Library.

ISBN 978 1 84255 148 6

Printed in Great Britain by Clays Ltd, St Ives plc

www.orionbooks.co.uk

Don't Cook Cinderella

Francesca Simon is the author of the best selling *Horrid Henry* books. She spent her childhood on the beach in California, and then went to Yale and Oxford Universities to study medieval history and literature. She now lives in London with her English husband and their son. When she is not writing books she is doing theatre and restaurant reviews or chasing after her Tibetan Spaniel, Shanti.

Tony Ross is the illustrator of the *Horrid Henry* books, and of hundreds of other books too, including his own picture books. He is one of the best-known children's illustrators in the world. He lives in Oxfordshire.

For Paula Hamilton
and Kate Lock
with love

Contents

Troll

Ugly Sister 1

Ugly Sister 2

Miss Bad Fairy

Goldilocks

Little Red Riding Hood

The Three Pigs

Miss Good Fairy

Magic Beans

Once upon a time, long long ago, in a land far far away, in olden days, when wishing was having, some children started school.

'Hello, everyone!' said the teacher. 'Welcome to your new school. Let's start with the register. Gretel?'

'Here, miss.'

'Hansel?'

'Here, miss.'

'No sweets in school, please,' said the teacher.

'Hansel, those are my sweets!' said Gretel.

'No they're not!' said Hansel.

'Mine!' said Gretel, snatching the gingerbread.

'Mine!' said Hansel, snatching it back.

'Children, stop squabbling,' said the teacher. 'Put those sweets away until after school. Cinderella?'

Silence.

'Cinderella?'

Silence.

The teacher made a mark in her register. 'Not here. Three little pigs?'

'Oink.'

'Oink Oink.'

'Oink Oink Oink.'

'Sleeping Beauty? Sleeping Beauty!'

A girl asleep on the carpet woke up.

'Yes, miss,' yawned Sleeping Beauty.

'Little Red Riding Hood?'

'Yes, miss.'

'Goldilocks?'

'Here, miss.'

'Snow White?'

2

Snow White
was smiling at
herself in a small
mirror. 'Here, miss.
Do you like my
new dress?'

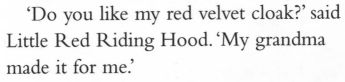

'Put the mirror
away, please, Snow
White. Your dress is
lovely,' said the teacher.

'Do you like my red velvet cloak?' said
Little Red Riding Hood. 'My grandma
made it for me.'

'It's lovely,' said the teacher. 'Jack?'

'Here, miss. I've got something for show
and tell – magic beans!'

'They don't look magic to me,' said
Goldilocks.

'They are magic!' said Jack. 'You'll see.'

'Please put them away,' said the teacher.
'You can show them later.'

'But I want to show them now,' said Jack.

3

'Later, Jack,' said the teacher. 'Well done, everyone!'

The door banged and a girl with a dirty face and dusty dress burst in, panting.

'Sorry I'm late,' she whispered. Then she began to cry.

'Come and sit next to me and tell me what happened, Cinderella,' said the teacher, handing her a hankie. The girl blew her nose.

'My stepsisters made me fetch the water and make the fire and cook and scour and I've only just finished,' she said tearfully.

'You're here now, that's the main thing,' said the teacher. 'Sit down on the carpet with the other children. I'm your teacher, Miss Good Fairy. I hope you'll all be very happy here, and learn to work hard, play fair, think for yourself, listen, and get along well together. Some of the big children may be a bit rough, but don't worry. You'll soon learn how to handle them.

'Now I want you to write a sentence about what you did in the holidays. Don't worry if you can't spell everything – I'll come round to help.'

The children sat at the tables and went to work.

Little Red Riding Hood leaned over to see what Jack was writing.

'Don't be so nosy, Little Red Riding Hood,' said Miss Good Fairy.

When they'd finished writing, everyone read their sentences aloud.

I visited my grandmother who isn't very well

My stepsisters made me pick peas out of the ashes

We got lost in the forest but Hansel dropped white pebbles on the ground and we found our way home again

I found a spinning wheel
in the ~~atic~~ attic

I met some dwarves and
worked very hard washing and
sewing and knitting

I found a little house in
the woods where three bears
live

Oink, Oink, Oink,
Oink, Oink, oink, Oink

'You built a big house out of straw.
Really!' said Miss Good Fairy.

Oink oink, oinky oinky,
oink.

'You built a great big house out of
wood! Fancy that!' said Miss Good Fairy.

oink, oink, oink OINK
oink OINKY OINK

'You built a great big giant house out of
brick! My goodness!' said Miss Good Fairy.

I swapped our cow for some magick beans

'Clever boy!' said Miss Good Fairy. 'I'll bet your mum was proud of you.'

'Actually, she got very cross,' said Jack.

'Oh dear,' said Miss Good Fairy. 'Never mind. What clever children you are! And what a lot of adventures. Keep up the good work, everybody. Now it's time for sums. Goldilocks, sit in your own chair, please! Gretel, if Hansel dropped ten breadcrumbs and the birds ate four, how many crumbs would be left?'

'Six,' said Gretel.

'Well done,' said Miss Good Fairy. 'Snow White, if there were seven dwarves, and five of them went to work, how many would be left?'

'Three?' said Snow White.

Goldilocks waved her hand wildly.

9

'I know, I know,' she shouted.

'Please raise your hand if you want to speak,' said Miss Good Fairy. 'Can you help her, Little Red Riding Hood?'

'Two,' said Little Red Riding Hood, leaning back in her chair.

'Correct,' said Miss Good Fairy. 'Be careful how you're sitting, Little Red Riding Hood, or you'll fall off and hurt yourself.'

Little Red Riding Hood paid no attention and leaned back even further. Gretel waved her hand.

'Miss! Miss!'

'Yes, Gretel?' said Miss Good Fairy.

'My tooth is wobbly,' said Gretel.

'Don't wobble it now, please,' said Miss Good Fairy.

CRASH!

Little Red Riding Hood fell off her chair. 'OWWWWWW,' shrieked Little Red Riding Hood.

'One day you'll get into trouble for not listening, Little Red Riding Hood,' said Miss Good Fairy, helping her up.

'I don't think so,' said Little Red Riding Hood merrily.

'Hmmn,' said Miss Good Fairy. 'Jack, if a magic hen laid four golden eggs on Monday and five golden eggs on Tuesday, how many eggs would she lay?'

'Eight?' said Jack.

'Not quite,' said Miss Good Fairy.

'Nine!' said Cinderella.

'Clever girl,' said Miss Good Fairy. 'Sleeping Beauty, sit up please!'

'Sorry, miss,' yawned Sleeping Beauty.

'Silent reading on the carpet, please,' said Miss Good Fairy.

C.A.T. Spells Dog

While the Infants were busy reading, another teacher was taking the junior register in the next class. She was cross because everyone had arrived late.

'Ugly Sister One?'

'Not here . . . ha ha ha!'

'Ugly Sister Two?'

'In the toilet!'

'Someone flush it quick!' said Ugly Sister One.

'Shut up, pimple-face,' said Ugly Sister Two.

'Shut up yourself,' said Ugly Sister

One, yanking her sister's hair. Ugly Sister
Two pulled hers back. Then they both
started screaming.

'Good work, girls!' said the teacher. 'I
see you've done your name-calling
homework. Wicked Stepmother?'

'Blehh!'

'Big Bad Wolf?'

'Awhooooooo!'

'Wicked Witch?'

'Go away!'

'Jealous Queen?'

Jealous Queen was too busy chatting
to her magic mirror to answer.

'Mirror, mirror on the wall,
Who's the fairest one of all?'

'Jealous Queen!'
'Shhh!' said Jealous Queen.

'Snow White is the fairest of them all,'
said the mirror.

'Rats!' screamed Jealous Queen.

'Troll?' said the teacher.

'Ugghhhh!' growled Troll.

Everyone was there except Giant, who had been suspended for bullying the Head.

'Good work, Bad Class,' shrieked the teacher. 'I hate classes that say "Here, miss," all nice and sweet when I take the register.'

The teacher walked round the room carrying a big cane, which she whacked on a desk every now and then as hard as she could.

'I'm your teacher, Miss Bad Fairy. I hope you'll all be very unhappy here and learn to be even meaner and nastier and viler than you are now. Troll, stop scratching!' she added, whacking the seat next to him. 'Keep your nits to yourself.'

'Grrr,' said Troll.

'Don't you use that tone of voice with me, young man,' snarled Miss Bad Fairy.

A spitball whizzed through the air. Miss Bad Fairy glared at her Class.

'Who threw that spitball?'

Silence.

'WHO THREW THAT SPITBALL!' shouted Miss Bad Fairy.

'I did,' said Big Bad Wolf. 'Wotcha gonna do about it?'

Miss Bad Fairy made a big black mark in her register.

'Keep up the good work, Big Bad Wolf! Go to the top of the class! As I was saying, before I was so rudely interrupted

–' she smiled at Big Bad Wolf – 'you'll learn how to trick children, how to build gingerbread houses, how to disguise yourself, and the perfect way to roast a child. Best of all, there are lots of little kids in the Infants to practise on!'

And she cackled happily.

'But first, before you gobble any children, you have to learn to read, write and add.'

'What!' shrieked Wicked Witch. 'I want to eat Hansel now!'

'I hate reading!' bellowed Troll.

'Who wants to add?' sneered Ugly Sister Two.

'My servants write for me,' said Jealous Queen.

'How are you going to cook Cinderella if you can't read a recipe?' roared Miss Bad Fairy. 'How are you going to curse long-distance if you can't write? How will you know how many

windows to put in a gingerbread house if you can't add?'

Wicked Stepmother raised her hand.

'Put that hand down, Wicked Stepmother!' barked Miss Bad Fairy. 'We shout out in this class! And you, Ugly Sister One! Pull your sister's hair harder!'

'I need a wee,' said Troll.

'Too bad,' said Miss Bad Fairy. 'Now get ready for some sums. Big Bad Wolf! If you ate Grandma, Little Red Riding Hood and the huntsman, how many people would you eat?'

Big Bad Wolf looked down at his paws.

'Uhhh,' he said.

'Come on, birdbrain! I haven't got all day.'

'Fifty?' said Big Bad Wolf.

'Wrong! How are you going to keep track of how many people you've eaten if you can't add? You'll be sick with a tummy ache before you can say, "The better to eat you with". What's the right answer, Troll?'

Troll frowned. 'I can only count to one,' he said.

Miss Bad Fairy sighed. 'Very disappointing, Troll. I expected more. Let's see if you're any better at reading. Jealous Queen! What does this say?'

Jealous Queen smiled at herself in her mirror.

'I don't know and I don't care.'

'You don't care?' cackled Miss Bad Fairy. 'Don't care indeed! Call yourself a Jealous Queen and you can't read the word poison. Disgraceful. Just remember, my girl:

> Don't care was made to care,
> Don't care was hung,
> Don't care was put in a pot
> And boiled till he was done.

'Now, who's my next victim?' rasped Miss Bad Fairy. Her red eyes scanned the classroom. 'Stand up, Big Bad Wolf. How do you spell "huff and puff"?'

Big Bad Wolf looked doubtful.

'XYJZ?' he said.

'Ninny!' shrieked Miss Bad Fairy. 'Troll! What does C-A-T spell?'

'Dog,' said Troll desperately.

'Idiot!' shouted Miss Bad Fairy.

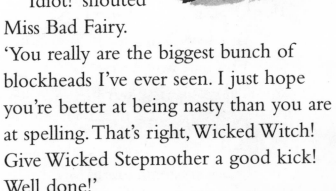

'You really are the biggest bunch of blockheads I've ever seen. I just hope you're better at being nasty than you are at spelling. That's right, Wicked Witch! Give Wicked Stepmother a good kick! Well done!'

'I've had enough of this,' said Big Bad Wolf. 'I want to eat the Infants.'

'Yeah!' said Troll.

'Then get to work on that alphabet!'
roared Miss Bad Fairy.

'What?' said Ugly Sister One in her
squeaky voice.

'What?' said Ugly Sister Two in her
gruff voice.

> 'What! What! Go to pot!
> Cat's tails all hot.
> You're an ass and I'm not,'

sneered Big Bad Wolf.

> 'Donkey walks on four legs
> And I walk on two;
> The last one I saw
> Was very like you!'

chanted Ugly Stepsister.

> 'Tell her! Smell her!
> Kick her down the cellar!'

snarled Big Bad Wolf, and chased her
screaming round the room.

What Troll Learned

While the Infants learned to read, write, add, and work together, Wicked Witch learned how to build a gingerbread house, Jealous Queen learned how to poison apples, Wicked Stepmother, Ugly Sister One and Ugly Sister Two

learned how to be even meaner and
viler, Big Bad Wolf learned how to

disguise himself, Troll
learned – well,

I'm not exactly sure what Troll learned.

Huff and Puff

Miss Bad Fairy blew her whistle sharply.
The gym echoed to the thud of running
feet.

'You're getting short of puff, Big Bad
Wolf!' shouted Miss Bad Fairy. 'Run faster!

You'll never blow down those pigs'
houses with that little breath! Huff and
puff, huff and puff, huff and puff! Just
look at you, Ugly Sisters! How do you
expect to dance all night at the ball if
you can't run sixty feet without panting?
Wicked Witch! Get those knobbly knees
moving! Troll! Pick up those big clompy
feet!'

'When . . . do . . . we . . . attack . . . the . . . Infants?' panted Wicked Witch.

'Soon,' said Miss Bad Fairy.

'When's . . . soon?' gasped Wicked Witch.

'When you're good and ready and not before!' screamed Miss Bad Fairy.

'But . . . I . . . want . . . to . . . crunch . . . some . . . children . . . NOW!' puffed Big Bad Wolf.

'Yeah . . . Food! Food!' panted Troll. 'Gimme . . . food!'

'Don't be fools!' shouted Miss Bad Fairy. 'We have to be clever about this.

When you've learned everything you
need to know, then we'll gobble them
up.'

'I'm ... not ... waiting ... any ...
longer,' muttered Wicked Witch.

'Me neither,' growled Big Bad Wolf.

'Yeah!' said Troll.

The bell rang.

LUNCHTIME!

5

Snakes and Snails
for Lunch

The Juniors pushed and shoved their way
into the lunchroom, where the Infants
were waiting in line.

'Food! Gimme food!' hissed Troll, licking his lips. He sneaked up on Sleeping
Beauty. But just as he was about to
pounce, the dinner lady looked up from
her cauldron.

'What are you doing?' said the dinner
lady.

'Nothing,' snarled Troll.

'Get back in line and wait your turn,'
said the dinner lady.

Troll shoved his way back into the
queue.

'Stop pushing,' said Jack.

Troll ignored him.

'Hit me! What did I say?' said Ugly
Sister Two.

'Hit me,' said Troll.

Ugly Sister Two slugged him.

'Owwwww!' whined Troll. 'Why did
you hit me?'

'You told me to,' said Ugly Sister Two.

'Grrrrrr,' said Troll.

'The choice today is turkey and peas or snakes and snails,' said the dinner lady.

'What? No roast children?' said Wicked Witch. 'I'll have to have the snakes, then.'

The dinner lady piled some on to her plate.

'Hmmmm, not bad,' said Wicked Witch, popping a fat juicy one into her mouth.

'Nothing for me. I'm on a diet,' said Jealous Queen.

'My mum won't let me eat vegetables,' said Troll.

'Don't you have porridge?' said Goldilocks.

'Not today,' said the dinner lady. 'What would you like, Cinderella?'

'Oh, whatever's left,' whispered Cinderella.

'Come on, dear, speak up for what you

31

want, turkey or snakes?' said the dinner lady.

'Turkey please,' said Cinderella.

'If you don't blow your own trumpet no one else will,' said the dinner lady. 'Remember that.'

Cinderella carried her plate to the table. Bad Class was hogging most of the bench so the Infants squeezed precariously on to the edge.

'This is the best meal I've had in ages,' said Cinderella, stuffing food into her mouth.

'Me too,' said Hansel, his mouth full.

'NOW!' said Ugly Sister One.

Bad Class shoved together.

CRASH!

The Infants fell off the bench on to the floor.

'OWWWWWW,' they wailed.

'Gimme that,' snarled Big Bad Wolf, snatching Gretel's plate.

'No!' cried Gretel.

Big Bad Wolf guzzled down all Gretel's food. Troll grabbed Hansel's plate and did the same. Hansel and Gretel burst into tears.

'We're hungry!' they cried.

'I'm not eating this swill!' said Ugly Sister One, throwing her plate at Cinderella.

'AAAAAAAGGGHHHHH!' cried Cinderella.

Bad Class pelted the Infants with food. Then they started throwing food at each other, screaming and laughing.

Miss Bad Fairy flew in. 'Keep up the good work, Bad Class,' she shrieked.

6

Help!

After lunch, it was playtime. The Infants walked quietly to the playground.

The Juniors didn't.

Jack walked round the secret garden, flipping his beans into the air. Big Bad Wolf sidled up to him.

'Hi! What you got there?' asked Big Bad Wolf.

'Magic beans,' said Jack.

'Oooh. Could I see them?' said Big Bad Wolf.

Jack hesitated. Big Bad Wolf gave him a beaming smile.

'Oh please. Pretty please. Pretty please with sugar on top.'

'All right,' said Jack, handing them over. 'Just for a minute.'

Big Bad Wolf snatched the beans and dashed away. 'Nah nah ne nah nah.'

'Give them back!' shrieked Jack.

Big Bad Wolf scampered off, then stopped. He started to hand the beans to Jack; then suddenly he threw them over his shoulder into the grass.

'Whoops! How clumsy of me,' said Big Bad Wolf. He strolled away, laughing.

'My beans! My beans!' cried Jack. He burst into tears and ran after him.

'Get away from me!' said Big Bad
Wolf, pushing Jack away. Jack fell. Big
Bad Wolf stood over him and began to
drool.

'Help!' shouted Jack.

Little Red Riding Hood ran over.

'Stop it! Leave him alone!'

'Go away,' snarled Big Bad Wolf.

'I said, LEAVE HIM ALONE!' said Little Red Riding Hood. She tugged at Big Bad Wolf.

'What's your name?' growled Big Bad Wolf.

'Little Red Riding Hood.'

'I'll catch you later,' said Big Bad Wolf. He tried to swagger as he walked away.

'Thanks for rescuing me,' said Jack.

'That's okay,' said Little Red Riding Hood. 'Race you to the shed?'

'Last one there's a rotten egg!' said Jack. They ran off, laughing, almost knocking over Hansel, who was pretending to be a pirate.

'I'm the captain! Obey me or else!' shouted Hansel. He thrust his sword at his enemy.

'I smell delicious tender flesh!' cackled Wicked Witch, sniffing hard. She peered

near-sightedly at Hansel. 'Who is it?'

'On guard, Bluebeard!' shrieked Hansel, waving his sword. 'Take that, you fiend.'

'Hansel!' hissed Wicked Witch. 'He won't escape me now. Little Hansel! Oh Little Hansel!'

'Yes?' said Hansel.

'Would you like some sweets?' asked Wicked Witch, holding out a chocolate bar.

'Yes, please!' said Hansel.

'I'm an old woman and I can't see very well,' said Wicked Witch. 'Come a little closer, my dear.'

Hansel came closer.

'I'm sorry, my dear, just a little closer,' said Wicked Witch.

Hansel came closer and reached for the chocolate. Wicked Witch grabbed him. Hansel tried to pull away but Wicked Witch was too strong.

'Gotcha, you tender little toad!' said
Wicked Witch. 'I can taste those plump
and juicy thighs already! Ugly Sister Two,
help me drag him to the woods.'

'Help yourself,' snarled Ugly Sister
Two, snapping her chewing gum. '*I'm*
looking for my ball.'

Wicked Witch started
dragging Hansel away.

'Wait a minute!' shouted Hansel.
'You're making a big mistake. I'm all skin
and bones. I'd taste terrible. Feel my leg.'

Hansel stuck out his finger.

Wicked Witch felt it. 'Uggh. Bony!'

'But Ugly Sister One over there – I
bet she'd taste great,' said Hansel.

'Ugly Sister One,' said Wicked Witch
doubtfully.

'She's much bigger and plumper and
juicier than I am,' said Hansel. 'I'm so
small and skinny I'd only be a mouthful.'

Wicked Witch peered at Ugly Sister
One's meaty arms and legs.

'Hmmmm. Maybe you're right.'

She let Hansel go and hobbled after
Ugly Sister One.

'GIVE ME MY BALL!' screamed Ugly
Sister One, running after her sister who
had snatched it.

'Where'd she go?' howled Wicked
Witch. 'Where'd she go? Ugly Sister!

Ugly Sister! Come back! Come back! Get out of my way, Troll!' she hissed, spitting at Troll, who was scuffling around by himself in the dirt and singing a little song.

Nobody loves me,
Everybody hates me,
What's a troll to do?
When I feel sad
and grumpy,
Pimply, grisly, plain
and bumpy,
There's only one
thing to do – think
I'll go and eat worms.

Big fat juicy ones,
Little squiggly
niggly ones.
Watch them wriggle
and squirm.
Going in the garden
To eat worms.

Bite their heads off,
Suck their guts out,
Throw the
skins away.
Nobody knows how fat I grow
On a hundred worms a day.

He stared at the ground.

'Gotcha!' said Troll, popping a worm in his mouth. 'Yum yum yum yum yum.'

'Troll!' said Jealous Queen. 'How would you like someone tender and juicy to eat?'

'Yeah!' said Troll.

'I thought so,' said Jealous Queen. 'Help me capture Snow White and she's yours.'

'Ahhh!' said Troll. He licked his lips.

'Now listen carefully,' said Jealous Queen. She whispered in his ear. 'Do and say exactly what I've told you.'

'Stop bossing me around,' said Troll.

'Shut up. She's coming,' said Jealous Queen. 'I'll hide by the gate.'

Jealous Queen hid herself as Snow White and Gretel walked past, chatting.

'I never want to grow up,' said Snow White. 'I'm happy just as I am.'

'Don't you want to be big and in charge?' said Gretel.

'No!' said Snow White.

Troll blocked their path.

'I've got a present for you, Snow White,' he said.

'What? What?' said Snow White. 'I love presents.' She held out her hand. 'Wait,' she said, pulling back. 'It's not something yucky, is it?'

'Yucky? You mean like . . . flowers?' said Troll.

'No,' said Snow White. 'Like a frog, or worms?'

'Worms!' said Troll. 'That's my best present.'

'Uggh,' said Snow White. 'Let's go, Gretel.'

They walked on. Troll dashed in front of them.

'No! It's not worms,' said Troll. 'A pearl comb for your beautiful hair.'

'Where? Where?' said Snow White.

'It's a trick,' said Gretel.

'Don't be silly,' said Snow White.
'Where?'

'Just outside the school gate,' said Troll.
'Come and I'll show you.'

'Don't go,' said Gretel. 'We're not
allowed to leave school.'

'Show me,' said Snow White, following
Troll.

'Go away, Gretel,' said Troll.

'No!' said Gretel.

'Stop following me, Gretel,' said Snow
White.

'Come on,' said Troll.

He led Snow White to the gate. Gretel
followed them.

'Where is my present?' said Snow
White, stopping.

'Come on. Just a little further,' said
Troll.

'Bring it to me here,' said Snow White.

'No!' said Troll, grabbing her. 'Come
on.'

Snow White struggled to free herself. 'Let go of me!'

'No!' said Troll. 'Jealous Queen said . . .'

'Jealous Queen!' shrieked Snow White. 'Let me go!'

Gretel stared behind Troll and started to wave.

'Mother Goose! Mother Goose! You're just in time!'

Troll dropped Snow White's arm. 'The Head! Where?'

Snow White and Gretel grabbed hands and escaped.

'Thank you, Gretel,' said Snow White.

'I don't see Mother Goose,' said Troll. Then the light dawned. Troll whacked himself on the head.

'Oops,' said Troll.

Jealous Queen ran over, carrying a rolled-up newspaper. She proceeded to thwack Troll with it.

'Dunce! Dummy! Blockhead! Nitwit!

Birdbrain! Booby! Numskull! Toad!'
shouted Jealous Queen.

Troll lumbered away as fast as possible.
Jealous Queen followed him, whacking
him as hard as she could.

The Perfect Way
to Roast a Child

When playtime was over, the Infants went straight to Miss Good Fairy to complain.

'Big Bad Wolf won't leave me alone!' said Little Red Riding Hood.

'Ugly Sister One pulled my hair!' said Cinderella.

'Wicked Witch dragged me!' said Hansel.

'Wicked Witch bit me!' said Gretel.

'Big Bad Wolf took my beans and Ugly Sister Two knocked me off the climbing frame,' said Jack.

'Jealous Queen pinched me and Troll grabbed me!' said Snow White.

'OINK OINK OINK,' said the Three Little Pigs.

'That's terrible,' said Miss Good Fairy. 'I'll have a word with Miss Bad Fairy. I'm sure she'll put a stop to it.'

'I think Miss Bad Fairy *wants* them to be bad,' said Cinderella.

'Nonsense,' said Miss Good Fairy.

'I'm sure I saw her cheering them,' said Jack.

'I'll see what I can do,' said Miss Good Fairy.

'Aprons on, everybody!' shouted Miss

Bad Fairy. 'It's cookery time.'

Bad Class assembled around the giant black cauldron, wearing red-striped butcher's aprons.

Miss Bad Fairy glared at them.

'If anyone comes in, remember we're baking gingerbread men,' she said.

Miss Bad Fairy reached into the cauldron and picked up a biscuit sheet covered with gingerbread men. Then she tossed it back in.

'Right. Lesson One. The perfect way to roast a child,' said Miss Bad Fairy.

'Finally, we learn something useful,' said Wicked Witch.

'First of all, don't waste your time on a skinny, scrawny child,' said Miss Bad Fairy. She pulled a scraggy doll out of the cauldron.

'Too skinny – yuck!' She tossed the doll behind her. '*This* is what you want,' she added, pulling out a big fat doll.

'Plump and juicy, plump and juicy, that's the secret. You can't expect a great meal if your ingredients aren't the best.'

'What happens if a child isn't plump and juicy?' said Wicked Witch.

'Easy,' said Miss Bad Fairy. 'You fatten it up in a cage. Then every day ask it to stretch out a finger so you can feel how fat it's getting.'

'Ah! Fatten them in a cage! I never thought of that!' said Wicked Witch.

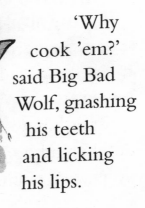

'Why cook 'em?' said Big Bad Wolf, gnashing his teeth and licking his lips.

'Yeah!' said Troll, gnashing his teeth, too.

Miss Bad Fairy sighed. 'I don't know why I bother with you lot, I really don't. Next, build —'

Big Bad Wolf interrupted. 'I think we should —'

Wicked Witch interrupted. 'Stop interrupting! This is the first good lesson we've had all year.'

Miss Bad Fairy continued. 'Next, build up a nice hot fire, and heat up the . . .'

'Mud!' said Troll.

'Snails!' said Big Bad Wolf.

'Twigs!' said Wicked Witch.

Miss Bad Fairy rolled her eyes. 'Wrong! How many times do I have to tell you to put water in the cooking pot!'

'Ahhh,' said Big Bad Wolf.

'Ahhh,' said Troll.

'Water! Ahhh,' said Wicked Witch.

'Then, when the water is boiling hot,

and flavoured with a turnip, or a carrot, or a spider, plop the little darling in!' said Miss Bad Fairy, throwing the plump doll in the pot. 'And don't forget to keep stirring.'

'I'm starving!' said Troll.

'When's lunch?' said Big Bad Wolf.

'When the child is cooked to perfection, you —'

'Eat!' said Troll.

'Wrong!' shouted Miss Bad Fairy. 'You get out a nice serving dish and bring your roast child to the table. Does anyone here know how to carve?'

'Carve?' said Troll.

'Carve?' said Big Bad Wolf.

'I do, I do,' said Wicked Witch. 'You just remember that . . .' and she started to sing:

> 'The head bone's
> connected to the neck bone,

the neck bone's
connected to the shoulder bone,
the shoulder bone's
connected to the backbone,
the backbone's
connected to the hip bone,
the hip bone's

connected to the thigh bone,
the thigh bone's
connected to the . . .'

Miss Bad Fairy interrupted. 'Yes, thank you, Wicked Witch. Are there any questions?'

'What about sauces?' said Ugly Sister Two.

'Ketchup!' said Troll.

'Ketchup? Bah. I'd chop off my cook's head if she served me ketchup,' sneered Jealous Queen.

'Mustard, hollandaise, pickle . . . the choice is yours,' said Miss Bad Fairy.

'I'm so hungry I could eat a child right now this second,' said Troll.

'Me, too,' snarled Big Bad Wolf. 'I'm fed up with school. When are we going to eat the Infants?'

'Yeah!' said Troll.

'Hansel is plump and juicy right now!

57

It was all your fault, Ugly Sister One, that he got away,' said Wicked Witch.

'It was not,' said Ugly Sister One.

'Yes it was,' said Wicked Witch.

'No it wasn't, it was your fault,' said Ugly Sister One. 'Anyway, it's not my job to help you, you ugly old crone. Help yourself.'

'Yeah!' said Ugly Sister Two.

'Cinderella wants to go to the ball,' said Ugly Sister One.

'The idea!' said Ugly Sister Two.

'The sooner we teach her a lesson the better,' said Wicked Stepmother.

'I'll help teach her!' said Troll, licking his lips.

'We all know how much your help is worth, Troll, after what happened yesterday,' sniffed Jealous Queen.

'Grrrr,' said Troll.

'I've had enough lessons,' said Jealous Queen. 'Snow White is getting lovelier

every day and I want to
poison her at once.'

'Poison her!' said Big
Bad Wolf. 'And spoil a
good meal!
You're
crazy.'

'Yeah!
Crazy!' said
Troll.

'Don't you call me
names, you mangy brutes. I'll poison her
if I want to,' said Jealous Queen.

'Go ahead then and see if I care,' said
Big Bad Wolf. 'There's plenty of plump
children to eat without that scrawny,
scraggy, stringy kid.'

'Snow White is not stringy! She's a
very attractive young girl – too attractive,'
said Jealous Queen.

'Ha!' said Big Bad Wolf.

Troll stamped his foot. 'I don't care if

she's fat or thin. Food is food.'

'I'm hungry,' said Big Bad Wolf.

'I'm hungry,' said Wicked Witch.

Bad Class stamped their feet on the floor.

'WHEN DO WE EAT THE INFANTS?!!' they shouted.

Miss Bad Fairy looked carefully around the room, peeping under the desks and behind the door, to make sure no one was listening.

'Today!' whispered Miss Bad Fairy.

Bad Class stomped, cheered, shouted and clapped.

Wicked Witch leaped on to the table and belted out:

'This time tomorrow, where shall I be?
Not in this academy!'

Then everyone joined in.

No more Latin, no more French,
No more sitting on a hard school
bench.
No more dirty bread and butter,
No more water from the gutter.
No more maggots in the ham,
No more yukky bread and jam.
No more milk in dirty jugs,
No more cabbage boiled with slugs.
Now's the time to say hurray.
We're eating the Infants today!

There was so much shouting that Miss Good Fairy popped in to see what all the noise was about.

'Any problem, Miss Bad Fairy?' asked Miss Good Fairy.

Miss Bad Fairy smiled sweetly. 'Oh no. Everyone's just excited about baking their gingerbread men.' Miss Bad Fairy waved the biscuit sheet ostentatiously.

'Could I have a word, Miss Bad Fairy?' said Miss Good Fairy.

'Certainly,' said Miss Bad Fairy. 'Class, practise your spells . . . spelling. How can I help, my dear Miss Good Fairy?'

'Your class is bullying my class.'

'How dare you?' snapped Miss Bad Fairy. 'My dear sweet little class – bullies? Never. Are you being bullies, class?'

'NO!' shouted Bad Class.

'There you are,' said Miss Bad Fairy. 'My class are not bullies.'

'Oh yes they are,' said Miss Good Fairy.

'Oh no we're not,' said Bad Class.

'OH YES THEY ARE,' said Miss Good Fairy.

'OH NO WE'RE NOT,' shouted Bad Class.

'OH YES YOU ARE!' said Miss Good Fairy.

'I've never been so insulted in my life,' said Miss Bad Fairy. 'Bullies indeed. How dare you talk to me like that?'

'I'll talk to you any way I want to,' said Miss Good Fairy. 'If you can't control your class's bad behaviour, I'm sure the Head can. Good day, Miss Bad Fairy.' She walked out the door and called out:

'Mother Goose! Oh Mother Goose!'

Miss Bad Fairy looked worried.

'Oh, Miss Good Fairy, why bother Mother Goose over such a little thing as my class hitting and pinching and tormenting yours?' said Miss Bad Fairy.

'Mother Goose! Oh Mother Goose!' called Miss Good Fairy.

'What am I saying?' said Miss Bad Fairy quickly. 'Have my big naughty brutes been bullying your sweet little teeny weeny darlings? That is terrible. I am shocked and appalled. Oh dear oh dear oh dear. What can I do?'

'Will you put a stop to it?' said Miss Good Fairy.

'Of course I will, dear Miss Good
Fairy,' simpered Miss Bad Fairy. 'There is
no bullying at this school. Thank you so
much for bringing this matter to my
attention.'

'Thank you,' said Miss Good Fairy.

'No, thank *you*!' said Miss Bad Fairy.

'No, no, thank you.'

'No, thank you!' said Miss Bad Fairy.

'Goodbye, Miss Bad Fairy,' said Miss
Good Fairy.

'Tootle-oo,' chirped Miss Bad Fairy.

'What a fool,' she added, when the door closed. 'Hee hee hee. Won't she be surprised when we gobble up the Infants!' 'Now listen carefully, Bad Class.' She took some papers out of her desk and unrolled them. 'Here are the plans . . .'

8

Plans for Gobbling up the Infants

It was playtime. Cinderella and Snow White sat talking while the others played skipping games. No one saw Miss Bad Fairy lean out of an upstairs window and count them.

'You're so pretty,' said Cinderella.

'I know,' said Snow White.

'I wish I were pretty,' said Cinderella.

'You are,' said Snow White.

'No I'm not. You're just saying that.'

'It's just a little hard to see under all those cinders,' said Snow White.

'I don't have a bed at home – my wicked stepmother and stepsisters make me sleep in the ashes,' said Cinderella.

'I had to leave home because my step-mother was so horrible to me. I got taken to the forest and left there,' said Snow White.

'No!' said Cinderella.

'I was. I live with seven dwarves now. I have to work awfully hard cooking and washing and knitting, and making all those beds.'

'Poor you,' said Cinderella.

'It's not so bad,' said Snow White. 'At least I'm safe from Jealous Queen there. Poor you.'

They smiled at one another. The others sang and skipped:

Up the ladder and down the wall,
Penny an hour will serve us all
You buy butter and I'll buy flour,

And we'll have a pudding in half an
hour.
With –
salt,
mustard,
vinegar,
pepper.

The Infants were so busy playing that
they didn't notice Big Bad Wolf, Troll and

Ugly Sister One sneaking up.

'Why don't we make some paper planes to throw at them?' hissed Ugly Sister One.

'Nah! Let's just eat 'em,' said Troll. He crept towards the Infants. Ugly Sister One grabbed his sleeve.

'Not yet, stupid! You'll spoil the plan!'

'Who are you calling stupid?' growled Troll.

'Who do you think?' said Ugly Sister One.

She took some rolled paper out of her pocket.

'I pinched this from Miss Bad Fairy's desk. It's nice and stiff,' said Ugly Sister One.

'It's got scribbles on it,' said Troll.

'Who cares!' said Big Bad Wolf.

Ugly Sister One, Troll and Big Bad Wolf folded their paper planes, making sure the tips were good and sharp and

pointy. Then they launched the darts at Miss Good Fairy's class.

'OUCH!'

'EEK!'

'OWWWW!'

'STOP!'

'NO!' shrieked the poor children, as the missiles landed. Big Bad Wolf, Troll and Ugly Sister One ran off, laughing.

Gretel wiped away her tears and picked up one of the darts from the ground.

'Look at this, it's got writing on it.'
The Infants huddled round.

'What does it say?' said Sleeping
Beauty.

'Pl–Pl–Plans . . . f . . . f . . .' began
Cinderella.

'For gob . . . gob . . .' read Gretel.

'Gobbling,' read Snow White.

'The In . . . What's the rest of that
word?' said Jack.

'In-fants,' read Hansel.

'Plans for gobbling up the Infants,' read Goldilocks.

They looked at each other.

'We'd better read the rest of this as fast as we can and tell Miss Good Fairy,' said Little Red Riding Hood.

Bags I the Pigs

Bad Class was in a flurry of excitement and preparation.

'Bags I the pigs!' shouted Troll.

'Bags I Red Riding Hood and the pigs,' said Big Bad Wolf.

'Bags I the pigs!' whined Troll.

'If you so much as touch them I'll huff and I'll puff and I'll . . .'

Troll backed away. 'Bags I Gretel.'

'Oh no you don't!' said Wicked Witch. 'Hansel and Gretel are mine.'

'You have Snow White, Troll,' said Jealous Queen.

'Okay,' said Troll sourly.

'We're sure to get her this time,' said Jealous Queen.

'Yeah,' said Troll.

'And Cinderella, too,' said Wicked Stepmother.

'Yum!' said Troll, licking his lips.

'Positions, everybody!' shouted Miss Bad Fairy, waving her flag. She handed out sacks, bibs, butterfly nets, and knives and forks. Bad Class tied the giant bibs around their necks.

'Is everybody ready?' said Miss Bad Fairy.

'YES!' shouted Bad Class.

'Do you all know what you're doing?' said Miss Bad Fairy.

'YES!!' roared Bad Class.

'Then let's get 'em!' shrieked Miss Bad Fairy. She waved her flag. Bad Class started stomping down the corridor.

'Shhh!' hissed Miss Bad Fairy.

75

Bad Class tiptoed down the hall to the
Infants. They stopped just outside the
closed door.

'When I give the signal,' hissed Miss
Bad Fairy, 'we burst in, grab 'em and stuff
'em in these bags.'

She swept down her starting flag.
'NOW!'

Wicked Witch flung open the door.
The room was dark.

'EEEEK,' she spluttered, as a bucket of water came down on her head. 'I'm melting!'

'AAAAGGGGGGHHH!' screamed the Ugly Sisters, as another bucket of cold muddy water landed on them. SPLAT!

Big Bad Wolf and Troll pushed in.

'Out of my way!' growled Big Bad Wolf.

'Whooooaaaa!' he
howled, skidding
on some marbles
and slamming into
a desk.
'OWWWW.'

'Out of my
way!' shouted
Troll. 'Ooops!'
he shrieked,
skidding on
more marbles
and crashing into a chair.

'What's going on in here? Attack I
say!' shouted Miss Bad Fairy. 'CURSES!'
she hollered, tripping over some string
and falling head first into the rubbish
bin.

'OUCH!' screeched Jealous Queen,
sliding on some slime and falling on top
of Troll.

'What are you
doing?' bellowed
Troll, shoving
her off.

'HELP!'
yelped
Wicked Stepmother, tripping over some
rope and

smashing into
Big Bad Wolf.

'Get off me,
you hag!'
growled Big Bad

Wolf, and bit her.

'Don't you call me hag!' yelled Wicked
Stepmother, biting him back.

'Leave me alone, you!' shouted Ugly
Sister Two, slapping her sister.

'Get away from me!' shouted Ugly
Sister One, yanking her hair.

CRASH! BANG! WALLOP!
THWACK! WHACK! SMACK!

A giant goose burst into the room.

'Stop it! What's going on in here?' she honked.

Bad Class froze.

'Mother Goose!'

Into the Woods

Bad Class, aching and sore, limped across the playground and staggered off into the woods.

'And never come back here again!' shouted Mother Goose.

Bad Class paused and shook their fists.

'Don't be too sure about that,' they hollered.

'Good work, children!' said Miss Good Fairy. 'I'm proud of you.'

'Congratulations, children,' said Mother Goose.

A large beanstalk suddenly sprang up

out of the ground.

'Mercy! What's that?' said Miss Good Fairy.

'My beanstalk!' said Jack. 'I told you my beans were magic!'

Jack started to climb.

'Watch out for giants, Jack,' said Miss Good Fairy.

'I'm not afraid,' said Jack.

'Good luck!' said Miss Good Fairy.

'Bye, Jack!' shouted the children, waving.

Then it was time for parents and guardians to pick up their children.

Cinderella's birds showered a beautiful ball dress on her.

'I'm going to the ball!' shouted Cinderella. She ran out of the gates, hugging her dress, singing and dancing, the birds fluttering around her.

'Come along,' said Hansel and Gretel's father.

'We're going into the forest to fetch wood,' said their mother.

Hansel and Gretel looked at each other fearfully.

'I'm scared,' said Gretel.

'We'll find some way out of this,' said Hansel. He reached into his pocket and dropped a white pebble on the ground. Then another, and another as Hansel and Gretel followed their parents into the forest.

Then an old woman appeared. 'Apples! Get your red, ripe, juicy apples!' she cried.

'Red apples!' said Snow White. 'My favourite. Old woman! Wait! Wait for me! I'll have one!' she shouted, running after her.

'Careful, Snow White,' said Miss Good Fairy. She started to follow her, then

stopped and let her go.

'How was school today?' asked Little
Red Riding Hood's mother.

'Okay,' said Little Red Riding Hood.

'What did you do?' asked her mother.

'Nothing,' said Little Red Riding
Hood.

'I want you to take this basket of food
and wine to your grandmother,' said her
mother. 'Don't dawdle, but don't run, or

you'll fall and break the bottle. And don't talk to strangers.'

Little Red Riding Hood took the basket. 'Don't worry. I'll do just as you tell me,' she said.